BOOTS &
THE GLASS MOUNTAIN

RETOLD BY
Claire Martin

PICTURES BY *Gennady Spirin*

DIAL BOOKS *New York*

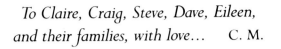

To Claire, Craig, Steve, Dave, Eileen,
and their families, with love... C. M.

For Ilya and Gennady G. S.

Boots and the Glass Mountain is based upon a Norwegian tale found in
many story collections, including *Popular Tales From the Norse* by Peter Christian
Asbjornsen and Jorgen Moe, published by David Douglas, Edinburgh, 1888.

Published by Dial Books for Young Readers • A Division of Penguin Books USA Inc.
375 Hudson Street • New York, New York 10014
Text copyright © 1992 by Claire Martin • Pictures copyright © 1992 by Gennady Spirin
All rights reserved • Typography by Amelia Lau Carling
Printed in the U.S.A.
First Edition
1 3 5 7 9 10 8 6 4 2

Library of Congress Cataloging in Publication Data
Martin, Claire.
Boots and the glass mountain / by Claire Martin ; pictures by Gennady Spirin.
p.   cm.
Summary: Boots saves his father's fields from the ravages of the trolls' wild stallions,
and with their help, he rides up the glass mountain and wins the princess's hand.
ISBN 0-8037-1110-7 (trade).—ISBN 0-8037-1111-5 (library)
[1. Fairy tales. 2. Folklore—Norway.] I. miirin, Gennadiĭ, ill. II. Title.
PZ8.M4447Bo   1992   398.2—dc20   [E]   91-9724   CIP   AC

Boots was scared. It was Midsummer Night, when ugly trolls and evil goblins roamed the Kingdom of the Glass Mountain. Tonight Boots had to stay alone in an old barn to guard his father's field.

Year after year on Midsummer Night some troll-beast or monster would come and eat as much grain in one night as a flock of sheep could eat in a month!

Two years ago Jon, the oldest brother, kept watch. But he came running home, too scared to scream.

Last year Nils, the middle brother, ran home too. Both times all the grain had been eaten away. Now it was Boots's turn to keep watch.

His brothers had made fun of him. "You won't catch anything," said Nils, "except maybe a cold!" At that they both laughed.

Boots was used to their teasing. Ever since their mother had died, they loved to torment him. He had the dirtiest chores to do, and he slept in the kitchen to tend the fire.

Now Boots reached for his tinderbox. It had been his mother's last gift to him. To pass the time, he took out the flint and a small piece of steel. Idly he tossed them up and down.

He remembered the day his mother gave the tinderbox to him. She had been so very ill. He had gone out early to pick flowers for her, but his clenched fist had crushed the stems, and his tears blurred their bright colors.

Then he had heard a musical voice: "What is it that troubles you?" asked a lovely young girl standing nearby. Her blue eyes had darkened as he told her, and she held out her own dew-fresh flowers. "For your mother," she said.

Then an older woman hurried the young girl away, exclaiming, "Just wait until your father the king hears about this!"

Boots's mother had brightened at the flowers, and had then given him the tinderbox. Boots blinked back tears now, recalling the touch of her hand.

Crash! A loud noise exploded, and the barn and the earth beneath it shook. Boots jumped. "If it doesn't get any worse, I guess I can stand it," he said aloud.

Bang! Another noise almost knocked him down, and the barn sagged. Boots was tossed from wall to wall, choking on dusty hay. He ran to the door, but stopped. "If it doesn't get any worse, I guess I can stand it."

Boom! He held his aching ears. The barn swayed and groaned. Boots was about to run…when the noise stopped. "I guess it will come again," he said. But everything was still. Then Boots heard a quiet chomp, chomp, chomp. Something was eating the grain! Ever so slowly he pushed open the barn door.

There stood the grandest horse he had ever seen.
It was pure white, with a gleaming copper saddle
and bridle. It carried a suit of copper armor.

The horse tossed its head, and stamped. Boots
stood frozen, clutching the flint and the steel.
Suddenly he remembered his mother's words: "It's
said that steel has power over troll magic." The horse
lowered its head and charged. Boots desperately
threw the steel.

At the metal's touch the animal stopped, then
trotted over to Boots as friendly as a puppy. It
nuzzled Boots's face. Boots laughed and picked up
the shining steel. Then he put on the armor and
rode his fine stallion away to a secret meadow that
only he knew about.

The next morning Boots was asleep by the kitchen fire. "Ha!" sneered Jon. "So, you were going to guard the field! Here you are, just as I said you'd be!"

"I suppose all our grain is gone too?" added Nils.

"Look for yourselves," Boots yawned, and went back to sleep.

His brothers walked out to the field and stared in amazement at the thick, swaying grain.

The following year Jon and Nils were still afraid to go out on Midsummer Night, so only Boots went. He waited eagerly in the shaking barn until he heard chomp, chomp, chomp. Outside stood a larger, grander horse, this one of chestnut color, with a silver saddle, bridle, and armor. Boots again tamed the horse with his steel, and rode it away to the secret meadow where he kept and cared for the first white stallion.

The following year Boots tamed the most beautiful horse of all, black as the night, with golden hooves. Its saddle and bridle and armor were purest gold.

Boots returned to the farm one sunrise, after tending his three stallions. His brothers were hitching the plow horse to the hay wagon.

"Where is it you go off to, whenever there's work to be done?" Jon demanded. Boots didn't answer him, but eased the horse into the traces.

"Where are you two going so early in the morning?" he asked.

"Why, it's the first day of the king's contest!" Nils answered. "We're going to see who will win the princess's hand!"

Boots turned pale, remembering the lovely young girl who had given him her flowers for his mother.

Jon laughed. "Yes, Boots, she's to marry whichever knight can ride up to the top of Glass Mountain."

"But I want to go too," pleaded Boots. "Let me go with you!"

"Nonsense," said Jon, picking up the reins. "There are still chores to be done!" He flicked the reins, and the old horse plodded through the gate.

The Glass Mountain had been made for the king by the Troll Chief. It was an evil gift for a foolish king, for with it the Troll Chief saw a way to gain the princess for himself.

Now that the young princess was seventeen, many suitors came seeking her hand in marriage. How could the king choose among them? The princess didn't seem to care for any of them. One day while gazing at his sparkling glass mountain, the king thought of a contest: The princess would sit at the top of the mountain, and the first knight or prince among her suitors who could ride his horse all the way up would win her hand!

The king asked the Troll Chief to build a staircase up the mountain so the princess could ascend. Then he gave his daughter three golden apples. The first knight to take the apples would be the winner.

The Troll Chief agreed to this. "But," he said, "if no one wins within three days, then the princess will be mine!"

"Oh, of course someone will win!" snapped the king. He sent out word of the contest far and wide.

When Boots's brothers joined the crowd at the Glass Mountain, the knights in bright armor and the princes in fine clothes were already charging their horses at its sides. But it was too steep and slick for even a lizard or a spider to climb. The horses pawed the glass, their hooves slipping. Those few that managed to get more than a couple of strides up, slid right back down again with a horrible screech. The princess was at the top, holding the apples of gold. Every prince and knight longed to win that prize.

Over and over they tried, until their horses were
exhausted.

As the sun dipped to the horizon, the king raised
his arm to end the contest for the day. But a murmur
went through the crowd. Galloping down the road
came a knight in brilliant copper armor, riding a fine
white horse.

The knight rode easily up the first part of the
mountain. Then he paused. He raised his visor and
waved to the princess, who stood up quickly. The
white horse began to slip. The girl threw down an
apple. The copper knight caught it as he turned and
rode swiftly away.

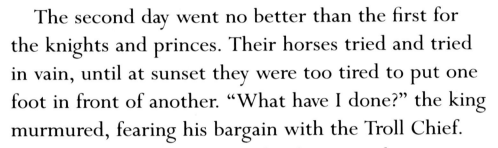

The second day went no better than the first for
the knights and princes. Their horses tried and tried
in vain, until at sunset they were too tired to put one
foot in front of another. "What have I done?" the king
murmured, fearing his bargain with the Troll Chief.

But the princess rose. In the distance a horseman
thundered toward the mountain. It was not the knight
in copper armor—this knight wore a suit of silver,
and rode a chestnut horse.

The silver knight rode easily up the first part
of the mountain. Then he conquered the second,
steeper part. He raised his visor and waved happily.
The princess smiled and waved too. But the silver
hooves slipped. The princess threw a second golden
apple. As the knight wheeled his horse, he caught it
and sped out of sight.

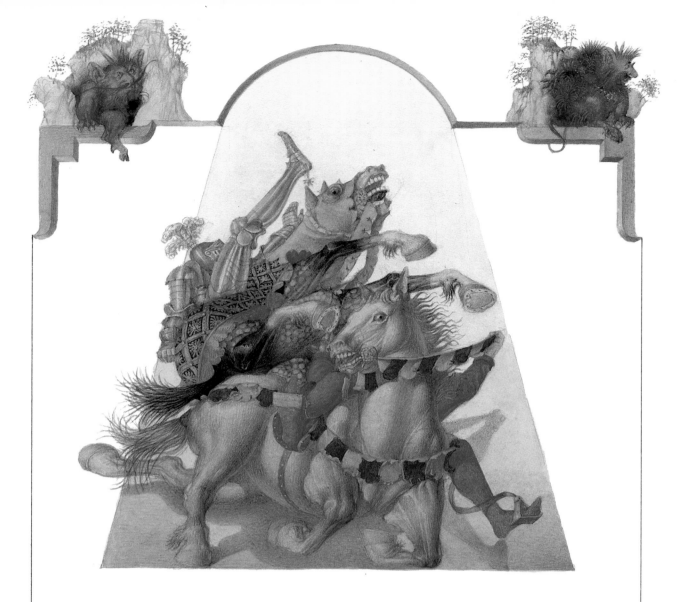

On the third and final morning the shoes of the knights' horses were well-sharpened, but all happened as before. The few who climbed a little farther up soon came screeching down again.

At dusk the ugly trolls, who feared the light, hid in the deepest shadows. They came out of their mountain caves to see their leader claim his bride.

The sun sank lower. The king and the crowd waited, listening. Finally they heard pounding hooves.

But the knight who galloped near was not the copper knight or the silver knight. This knight had armor of the purest gold. His midnight-black horse was the largest, grandest, and most beautiful that anyone had ever seen.

The crowd cheered the golden knight as he swiftly ascended to the very top of the Glass Mountain. He tipped his visor and took the third apple from the princess's hand. Then he swept her onto his saddle.

He eased the horse down the mountain, and set the princess into the waiting arms of her father, who hugged her tightly, saying, "I feared I had lost you forever."

The Troll Chief ran from the shadows with a cry of rage. As the golden knight turned, the sun's last rays caught his armor. The light glanced off and struck the troll, who was instantly turned to stone.

Then the Glass Mountain itself vanished, even before the other trolls could creep back into their caves, and the golden knight galloped away.

The next morning each knight and prince appeared before the king and his court. None could show even one golden apple.

"Summon every man in the kingdom!" proclaimed the king. Boots's brothers were the last to arrive.

"Who among you has a golden apple?" the king demanded.

No one answered. "Is there no one else at all to come before me?" he sighed.

"Well," said Nils, "there is our youngest brother."

"But he hasn't stirred from the hearth these last three days," Jon added.

"Bring him at once!" roared the king.

So Boots was brought in his tattered rags.

"I guess you don't have a golden apple, either!" the king said.

The princess, who knew Boots instantly, hid her smile.

"Do you mean these, sire?" Boots asked, drawing from his pockets one, two, three golden apples.

The brothers stared, for once speechless.

Boots then threw off his rags, and stood tall and
handsome in his suit of golden armor.

The princess ran to his side, and even a foolish
king could see their love.

A grand wedding was held. The whole countryside was there, and all the brave knights and handsome princes. Boots's brothers came too. Shamefaced, they shook Boots's hand, and wished him and his beautiful bride a long life of happiness and joy.